DATE DUE			

T98-291

E
YOL

Yolen, Jane.

Tea with an old dragon : a story of Sophia Smith, founder of Smith College

$13.54

Tea ^{with} ^{an} Old Dragon

Tea with an Old Dragon

A Story of Sophia Smith, Founder of Smith College

by Jane Yolen
Illustrated by Monica Vachula
Foreword by Ruth J. Simmons, President of Smith College

BOYDS MILLS PRESS

" . . . it is God's greatest pleasure that we should celebrate our lives."
—Sophia Smith, from her journal

For my Smith classmates of 1960 and for the following members of the Smith College community,
with thanks for their help and encouragement in the researching and writing of this book:
Dr. John Connolly, Dean of the Faculty; Margery Sly, former College Archivist and Coordinator of Special Collections;
Rachel Moore, Office of College Advancement; and Dr. Michael Gorra, Associate Professor of English.
—J.Y.

For George
—M.V.

Published by Caroline House
Boyds Mills Press, Inc.
A Highlights Company
815 Church Street
Honesdale, Pennsylvania 18431

Printed in Mexico

Publisher Cataloging-in-Publication Data
Yolen, Jane.
Tea with an old dragon: a story of Sophia Smith, Founder of
Smith College / by Jane Yolen ; illustrated by Monica
Vachula ; foreword by Ruth J. Simmons, President of Smith
College.--1st ed.
[32]p. : col. ill.; cm.
Summary: A young girl is befriended by Sophia Smith, who
later founded Smith College in Northampton, Massachusetts.

ISBN 1-56397-657-9

1. Smith, Sophia, 1796-1870--Juvenile biography. 2. Smith
College--Juvenile biography.
[1. Smith, Sophia, 1796-1870--Biography. 2. Smith College--
Biography.] I. Vachula, Monica, ill. II. Title.
092 [B]--dc21 1998 AC CIP

Library of Congress Catalog Card Number 97-72773

First edition, 1998
Book design by Amy Drinker, Aster Designs
The text of this book is set in 14-point Janson.
The illustrations are done in oil on Masonite.

10 9 8 7 6 5 4 3 2 1

Sophia Smith

A Greeting from the President of Smith College

We at Smith College, the nation's largest college for women, are rightly proud of our founder,
Sophia Smith of Hatfield, Massachusetts (1796-1870). Indeed, we just finished celebrating the
two-hundredth anniversary of her birth. One delightful aspect of the celebration has been the collaboration between two
of our accomplished alumnae, Jane Yolen and Monica Vachula, which has resulted in this wonderful book.

Jane and Monica have captured much of what we know about Sophia Smith: her advanced age (she was over
seventy at the time of the incident related in these pages), her deafness (she started to lose her hearing when she was forty years old),
the piano in her home on Main Street in Hatfield (we now have that piano on campus), her concern with being thrifty (a characteristic
of the Smith family), yet her great generosity, too. For Sophia Smith used her wealth to benefit countless people she would never
know: the students at Smith Academy in Hatfield and those at Smith College in Northampton, since both institutions were founded
with funds from her estate. The College alone has graduated close to fifty thousand women in its nearly 125-year history.

I hope you will enjoy reading this marvelous and beautifully illustrated story of a courageous little girl and the
mysterious "old dragon" she dared to visit one day long ago.
The spirit which each of them manifested deserves to be celebrated.

RUTH J. SIMMONS, President, Smith College

October 1867

William and I were on the front lawn, keeping an eye on our two-year-old brother, Harvey, the day I spoke to the Dragon. Harvey would have run into the road to fright the horses had we let him.

Three older boys went running by, slingshots tucked into back pockets, as if they had been up to some mischief. They shouted at us, "Look out! Better hide! The Old Dragon is coming!"

William dragged Harvey onto the front porch. But I did not run away. Though I was but six—well, almost—I was never such a frightened fool.

Besides, I would have loved to see a dragon.

Papa says it is not ladylike to wish for such things. And my brothers all smile behind their hands when he lectures me, which is—alas—far too often.

But I do not care. I believe in being honest. Papa is a minister and he should revere honesty. I do not think he reveres it in me.

Still I desired greatly to meet that dragon, so I peered down the street to see what had frightened the boys.

And there came Miss Sophy driving her big carriage, whipping past the Great Elm and on up the road. She was wearing a fine black dress with lace at the collar, and a white woolen shawl, seeming both stern and proud. On her head, as Papa would say, was thirty bushels of rye, so expensive was her hat.

But I didn't see any dragon, which was most disappointing.

Dust from the passing carriage got up my nose and I sneezed three times. When I had recovered, the carriage had turned onto Middle Lane and was gone beyond sight. And there was no one else—dragon or wagon or man on a horse—to be seen.

When we were all at lunch, I told Mama there was a dragon on our road. Three boys had said so, though only Miss Sophy had passed by.

Mama said sharply, "Louisa, do not call Miss Sophia Smith a dragon. Why, she is the finest woman in Hatfield."

My brothers laughed at that. Even baby Josie smiled.

But I replied, "I did not say *she* was the dragon, though my friend Emma calls her a terror. Emma says Miss Sophy near froze her with a look in church when she stepped on the tail of Miss Sophy's dress *purely* by accident."

Mama replied by sending me to my room without a bit of my noon meal, which seemed most unfair. There I was supposed to think about gossiping women and read several lessons in my Bible.

The Bible says little about dragons but much about women, which was a great disappointment. I was not let out again till near three.

When William came to tell me my punishment was over, I got out of the house as fast as I could for I did not want to mind Harvey again. Besides, I was determined to find the old dragon.

Since I did not know where else to start, I ran to Miss Sophy's house. She had been on the road the same time as the dragon. Surely if anyone knew where such a beast was, it would be the finest woman in town. And—people said—the richest, at least since her brother Austin died, leaving her his fortune. Everybody in Hatfield knew about Austin Smith, who wanted to take his money with him when he died but couldn't.

Miss Sophy's new house was across the street and up a ways from ours, sitting right by her old one. It was not at all like the rest of the houses on the road, with their white clapboards and dark shutters. Rather, it looked to have sprung from some other place than Hatfield, with a roof that sloped like a farmer's hat. Folks said it had marble fireplaces and wallpaper in every room!

I stood a long time at the front door, for suddenly I feared to knock. Then I heard Mama's voice down the road, calling my name. So I reached up but failed to touch the knocker by many inches. I had to bang my bare knuckles on the door, which is most unladylike, I am sure Papa would say.

For a minute I heard nothing. Then heavy footsteps came toward me and the latch was lifted, the door swinging inward.

"Yes?" a woman asked. "Who is calling?"

She was certainly not Miss Sophy. For one thing she was not nearly so old. Nor was she so well dressed. She wore a plain dark gown with a stained apron, and her cap was all awry. She was scowling. For a moment I thought *she* was the dragon. I almost turned to run. Yet I did not dare leave without answering her, though my heart beat as loud as a drum.

"I am Louisa Greene," I said. "I have come to find the old dragon."

At that the woman began to laugh, a short sharp bark that ended as quickly as it began. Then she pulled me right into the house.

"I have heard herself called many things," the woman said, "but never that!"

The door slammed shut behind me with a bang.

"Sarah? Sarah? Where *have* you got to?" called a voice from the back of the house. It was loud and booming, clearly a dragon's voice. "You have used an egg in the ginger loaf again, wicked girl. You will beggar us yet."

"The Old Dragon herself," whispered Sarah, winking at me. "Better beware." Then she turned and, speaking quite loudly, said, "You have a visitor who might appreciate a bit of egg to moisten that bread."

"I am expecting no visitors today," the Dragon said in a voice still unnaturally loud, though very near. "And I heard no one at the door."

That voice made me tremble.

Sarah moved aside then, and instead of a dragon, there was a small, elderly lady with a round face and bright eyes staring at me.

"And who are you?" the old lady asked in that loud dragon voice.

Suddenly I could not speak. The old lady *was* the dragon.

"Your visitor, Miss Sophy," Sarah said for me.

Miss Sophy! I had never actually been face to face with her before, except once in the sanctuary of my father's church. She looked exceedingly fierce, and my trembling became a shaking.

At that the Dragon walked toward me and did a most surprising thing. She took my chin in her hand and said, almost softly, "Ah—unexpected company is the sweetest. But wait here, child, till I get my tube."

And with a rustle of silk, she was gone.

Sarah went right after her, and I was left alone in that big front hall, dark as a dragon's lair, with a long, sweeping black wood staircase rising ahead of me to an even darker second floor.

It was autumn but the house was warm. Nevertheless, I continued to shiver. I thought about Papa and Mama and I thought about prayer. Then I thought long and hard about dragons.

What did Miss Sophy mean by saying that unexpected company was the sweetest? Did she plan to devour me?

And what had she meant by her *tube?*

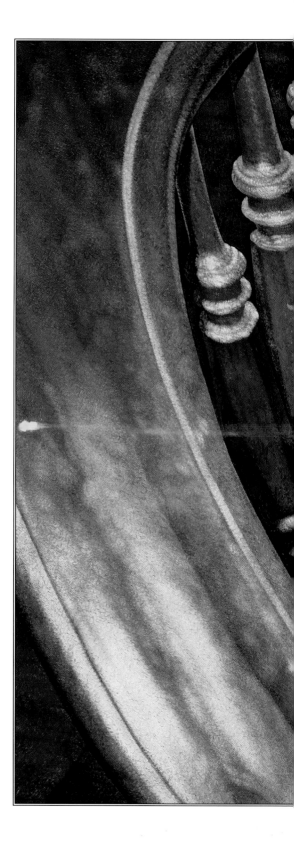

I shrugged out of my cape but had little time to contemplate my fate, for Miss Sophy returned almost at once. She carried with her a long brown tube that had a black hook on one end, a black cup on the other. Putting the hook right into her ear, she said loudly, "Now, child, place your mouth to the wide end. All that you say will be magnified. I have been calamitously deaf since I was forty."

That seemed the very definition of ancient to me. "How old are you now?" I asked, suddenly finding my tongue.

"Speak into the tube," she ordered.

I did so at once. One must never anger dragons.

"How are your sums?" she countered loudly. "I was forty past thirty-one years ago."

But such counting was as yet beyond me. When she saw me trying to add upon my fingers, she said, "I am seventy-one, child."

"Is that old for a dragon?" I shouted into the tube.

She smiled. "Quite old."

She took me by the hand and pulled me through the house. "Sarah will have sliced the ginger loaf. Be wary of her. She is a tyrant. Last time I scolded her about her baking, she threw an egg right at me!"

"Did it smash?" I shouted.

"All over the kitchen floor. She had to clean it up. But being deaf, I did not have to listen to her complaints." She laughed and it was such a nice sound, I was suddenly no longer afraid.

That is why, when we passed the Chickering by the white marble fireplace, I dared to ask loudly, "If you are deaf, why do you have a piano?"

"For my guests," she answered.

I could scarce believe it. "Am I a guest?" I whispered.

I had not shouted my question or even spoken it into the tube. But she seemed to read my thoughts. Dragons can do that, you know.

"Would you like to play, child?" she asked.

She led me to the piano and raised the lid. I stood for a long moment just staring down at the keys. How I longed to touch them.

"Go ahead, child," Miss Sophy commanded. "Make as much noise as you would like."

I took a deep breath and reached out a tentative finger.

One finger, one note.

Two fingers, two notes.

And then I let all ten fingers crash down upon the keys.

How I played.

Deep notes for the Dragon.

Splatting notes for Sarah and the egg.

Soft notes getting louder, and louder, and louder still for Miss Sophy herself.

Miss Sophy listened through her ear tube and occasionally clapped her hands.

When I was done, we went into the kitchen to have ginger loaf from the silver cake basket and honey tea in porcelain cups.

Miss Sophy let me wear her lace cap. It had wide lavender streamers. I recited Bible verses and a poem about a little lamb into her tube. In turn Miss Sophy recited the whole of the catechism *backwards*—both questions and answers. How we laughed at that!

Miss Sophy said I should come each day to play on her piano. "For whatever you most want to do, you must do with all your might."

"My father might not approve," I answered into her tube. "He rarely approves of the things I most want to do."

"Oh, Reverend Greene will listen to me," Miss Sophy said, "in the end. You can be certain of that." There was a bit of fire in her eyes when she said this, as if she really *was* a dragon. Then she added, "You shall have your piano lessons. For a girl needs to learn many things besides counting on her fingers, reading her Bible, and reciting one long poem about a little lamb."

"Even more than the catechism backwards?" I asked.

"Even more than that," she said.

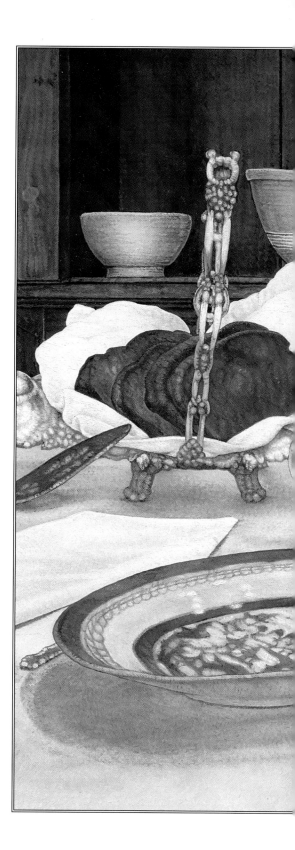

Every day but the Sabbath that cold winter, I bundled up with a scarf over my ears and mouth to go up the street to play Miss Sophy's piano. Every day, that is, till February when we left Hatfield and moved far away, for Papa had been given a bigger church. I am sure it was best for the family, but I cried for many days and would not be comforted.

I never saw Miss Sophy again. But I certainly heard much about her, eavesdropping as I shouldn't have at Papa's study door. For even though we had left Hatfield, Papa remained her advisor.

"Still, she does not always listen to me," Papa complained to Mama.

"She is deaf, dearest," Mama answered.

But I knew it was not the ear tube that kept Miss Sophy from always hearing what Papa had to say. Rather it was her fierce dragon's heart. This I knew, though Papa and Mama did not.

She had said as much to me that first day, her sharp eyes smiling into mine. "A girl needs to acquire wisdom and learn to think." Then, when she had served me another piece of ginger cake, she had added, "Especially a bold little girl like you, who dares come up the long street to have tea with an old Dragon."

What Is True About This Story

Reverend John M. Greene had four sons and two daughters, and one of them—Louisa—was allowed to play the splendid Chickering grand piano in Miss Sophia Smith's house. Helen French Greene—the younger sister, who was not born until ten months after the family moved away—related that surprising fact to a Smith College archivist in 1941. The archivist was collecting what little material existed about the college's founder, Sophia Smith.

The stories about Emma treading on Sophia Smith's dress, Sophia Smith complaining about the ginger cake, the irrepressible Sarah throwing an egg, the thirty-bushels-of-rye hat (though it was actually Sophia Smith's father who described it as such), the backwards catechism, the ear tube into which a child recited a poem for her, and Austin Smith's desire to keep his money even after death all come from the Hatfield, Massachusetts, traditions that have grown around Miss Sophy, as she was called by her neighbors. But besides those stories, her will, and a spiritual journal that she had kept during the last years of her life, there is precious little information about Miss Sophy except that she was the first woman to establish a genuine college for young women. Whether she was fiercely independent—as new research seems to suggest—or retiring—as others long believed—that fact alone makes her important in America's history.

Sophia Smith was Hatfield's richest lady because of the fortune left to her by her father, her uncle Oliver, and her brother Austin. She was a believer in higher education for girls, though she hardly had any schooling herself. It is said that as a girl she sat on the primary-school steps listening to the boys reciting their lessons inside. After consultation with Reverend Greene and others, all of whom had different ideas about what she should do with her money, she decided to leave the bulk of her fortune to found Smith College for young women so that they might restore their "usefulness, happiness, and honor."

The college was not established in Hatfield, where she had lived all her life, but in the neighboring city of Northampton. It had, among other amenities to recommend it, a railway station. At first the Hatfield folk thought to contest the will. But because Miss Sophy also had left a good deal of money to Hatfield for a secondary school for both boys and girls, they decided to leave well enough alone.

Today Smith College, with an enrollment of twenty-seven hundred women, is considered one of the leading colleges in the United States. Its graduates have become doctors, lawyers, actors, bankers, musicians, mathematicians, historians, scientists, diplomats, educators, social workers, and artists and writers like Monica Vachula and me. —J.Y.

The Sophia Smith Rose